BRAVE JACK

by Dave and Julie Saunders

Bradbury Press   New York

Maxwell Macmillan International
New York   Oxford   Singapore   Sydney

Jack sat up in the daisy field.

"How hungry I am!" he said. "Tonight
I will go to the big cabbage patch. Tonight
I will feast on cabbages. I'll visit my friends
on the way."

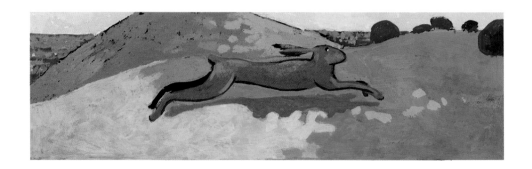

For Penny and David

First American edition
Text copyright © 1993 by Julie Saunders
Illustrations copyright © 1993 by Dave Saunders

Bradbury Press
Macmillan Publishing Company
866 Third Avenue
New York, NY 10022

Macmillan Publishing Company is part of the
Maxwell Communication Group of Companies.

First published 1993 in Great Britain
by Frances Lincoln Limited, Apollo Works
5 Charlton Kings Road, London NW5 2SB
with the title *The Brave Hare*

10 9 8 7 6 5 4 3 2 1

Library of Congress Cataloging-in-Publication Data
Saunders, Dave, date.
Brave Jack / by Dave and Julie Saunders. — 1st American ed.
p.   cm.
Summary: Despite the fears of his farmyard friends, Jack the
rabbit ventures into the cabbage patch.
ISBN 0-02-781073-9
[1. Rabbits—Fiction.   2. Animals—Fiction.]   1. Saunders, Julie.
II. Title.
PZ7.S253Br   1993
[E].   dc20   92-23238

Jack leapt through the fields. The sun was low in the sky as he raced down to the farm.

First he came to the kitchen door where Cat was lapping up her milk.

"Cat," said Jack, "I am going to the big cabbage patch to feast tonight."

"You can't do that!" said Cat. "A wicked old man guards that patch—you mustn't go there."

Jack just twitched his nose.

Jack and Cat came into the orchard where the Hen family was pecking for food.

Cat said, "Jack is going to the big cabbage patch to feast tonight."

"Oh, no, no, no!" the Hens clucked. "A fierce farmer guards that patch—you mustn't go there."

Jack just twitched his ears.

Goat was in the field, finishing dinner.

Cat said, "Jack is going to the big cabbage patch to feast tonight."

"Oh, no!" bleated Goat. "An enormous giant guards that patch—you mustn't go there."

Jack just twitched his paws.

The sun was setting when Jack and his friends found Goose nibbling the long grass by the barn.

Cat said, "Jack is going to the big cabbage patch to feast tonight."

"Oh, no!" honked Goose. "A terrible creature guards that patch—you mustn't go there."

Jack just twitched his tail.

It was beginning to grow dark but Pig was
still eating dinner. He looked up, surprised.
"Why are you all here?"

Cat said, "Jack is going to the big cabbage
patch to feast tonight."

"Oh, no!" grunted Pig. "A great flapping
monster guards that patch—you mustn't
go there."

Jack just twitched his whiskers.

"Well, I am going," Jack laughed. "I'll be brave. Wicked old men, fierce farmers, enormous giants, terrible creatures, and great flapping monsters don't bother me. Follow, if you dare!"

The animals looked anxiously at each other. "Shall we go?"

"We must," said Pig, "or Jack will think we're frightened. We must show we are brave, too."

Jack led the way, and his friends followed—
through the hedge and over the dark land.

At last they reached the edge of the big cabbage patch.

"Stay here!" said Jack. "I'll be brave. I'll go to the cabbage patch and see who's there."

The other animals huddled together. What was going to happen?

Jack bounded through the cabbages to
the feet of . . .

a scarecrow!
   "Come on," Jack yelled.
They all crept forward
to look, while Jack feasted
on the crispest cabbages
he had ever tasted . . .
   . . . crunch, crunch, crunch.